D0719170
PLEASE RETURN TO
503/4 THE CHAMBERS
CHELSEA HARBOUR · LONDON SW10 0XF
TELEPHONE: 0171 - 344 1000
FAX 0171 - 352 7356 · 0171 - 351 1756
PETERS
FRASER
&
DUNLOP

CROW AND HAWK

For Helen
Special thanks to Jackie Fortey and Alison Moss
for their help with this book
J.C.

Storyteller's Note

This story was told by an old Native American woman, well-known amongst her people, living in Cochiti, New Mexico. She belonged to a people that are sometimes called Pueblo Indians and the language that she spoke is Keresan. She told the story to a story-collector called Ruth Benedict, who, sadly, did not tell us her name.

Alfonso Ortiz, who wrote the introduction to this and other stories when they were published in 1981, says that the story was of the kind 'learned by the fireside during long autumn and winter evenings as a normal part of growing up'.

When you read the story you might like to think about who you think is right - Crow or Hawk? Or you might want to think about whether it was a good idea for them to go to see Eagle about the problem - was there any other way they could have sorted it out?

Michael Rosen

Acknowledgement

This story has been adapted from Ruth Benedict's
Tales of the Cochiti Indians, first published in 1931 and republished by
the University of New Mexico Press, Albuquerque, in 1981.

First published in 1995 by Studio Editions Ltd,
Princess House, 50 Eastcastle Street, London W1N 7AP, England

ISBN 1 85891 143 5

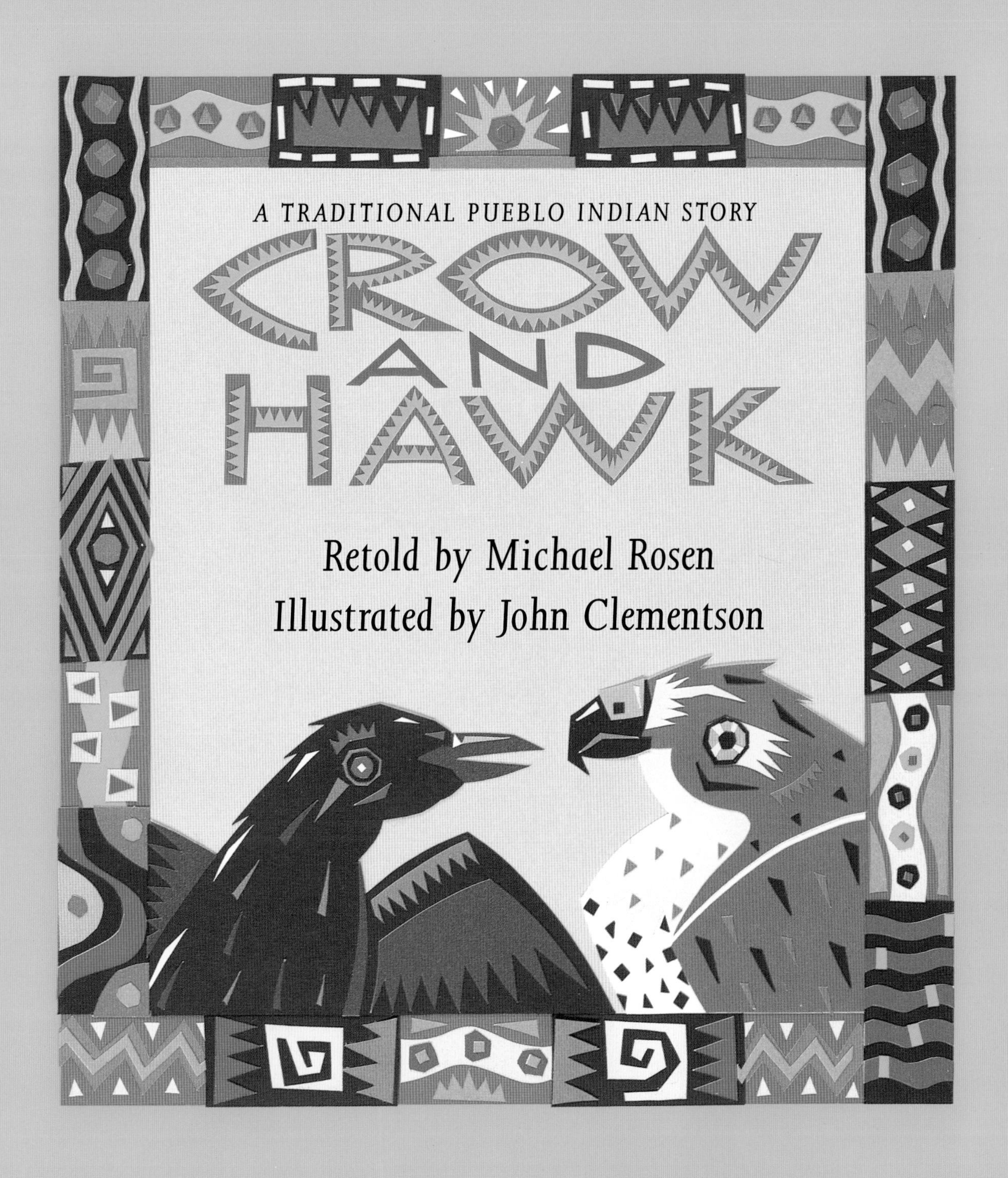

STUDIO EDITIONS
London

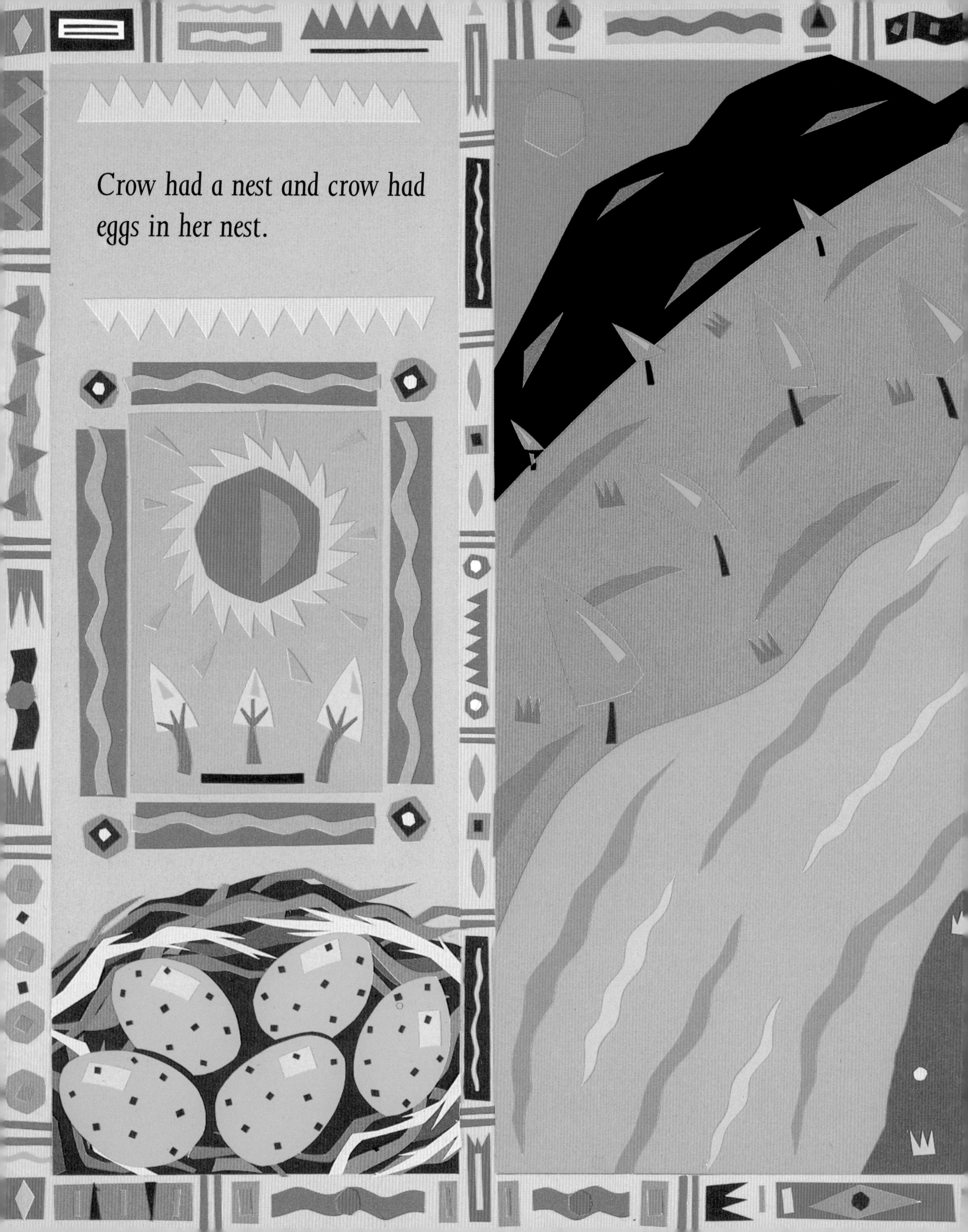

Crow had a nest and crow had eggs in her nest.

She sat and sat and sat.
Nothing happened.

She sat and sat and sat.
Nothing happened.

Crow got tired of all this sitting and sitting, so she flew away.

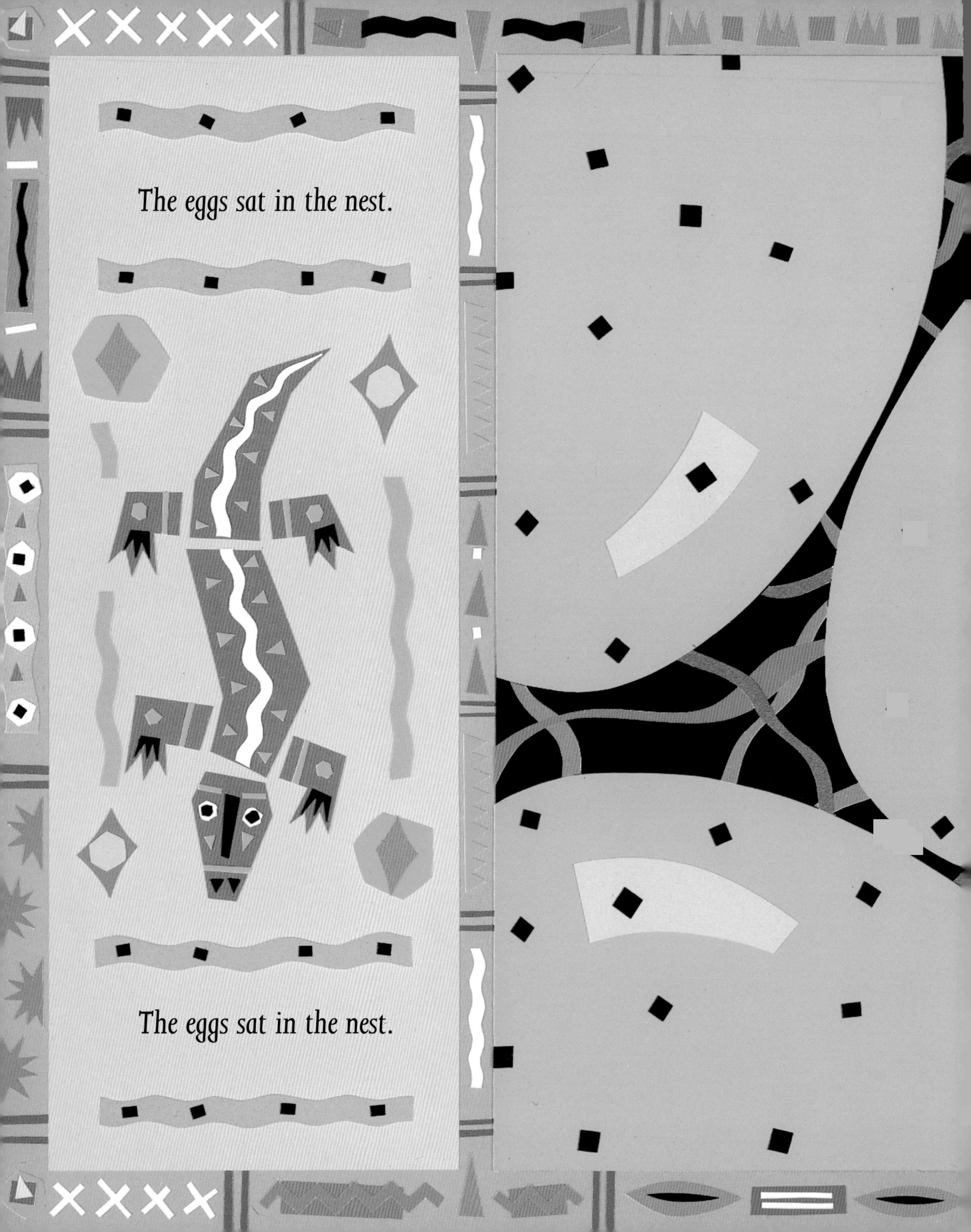
The eggs sat in the nest.
The eggs sat in the nest.

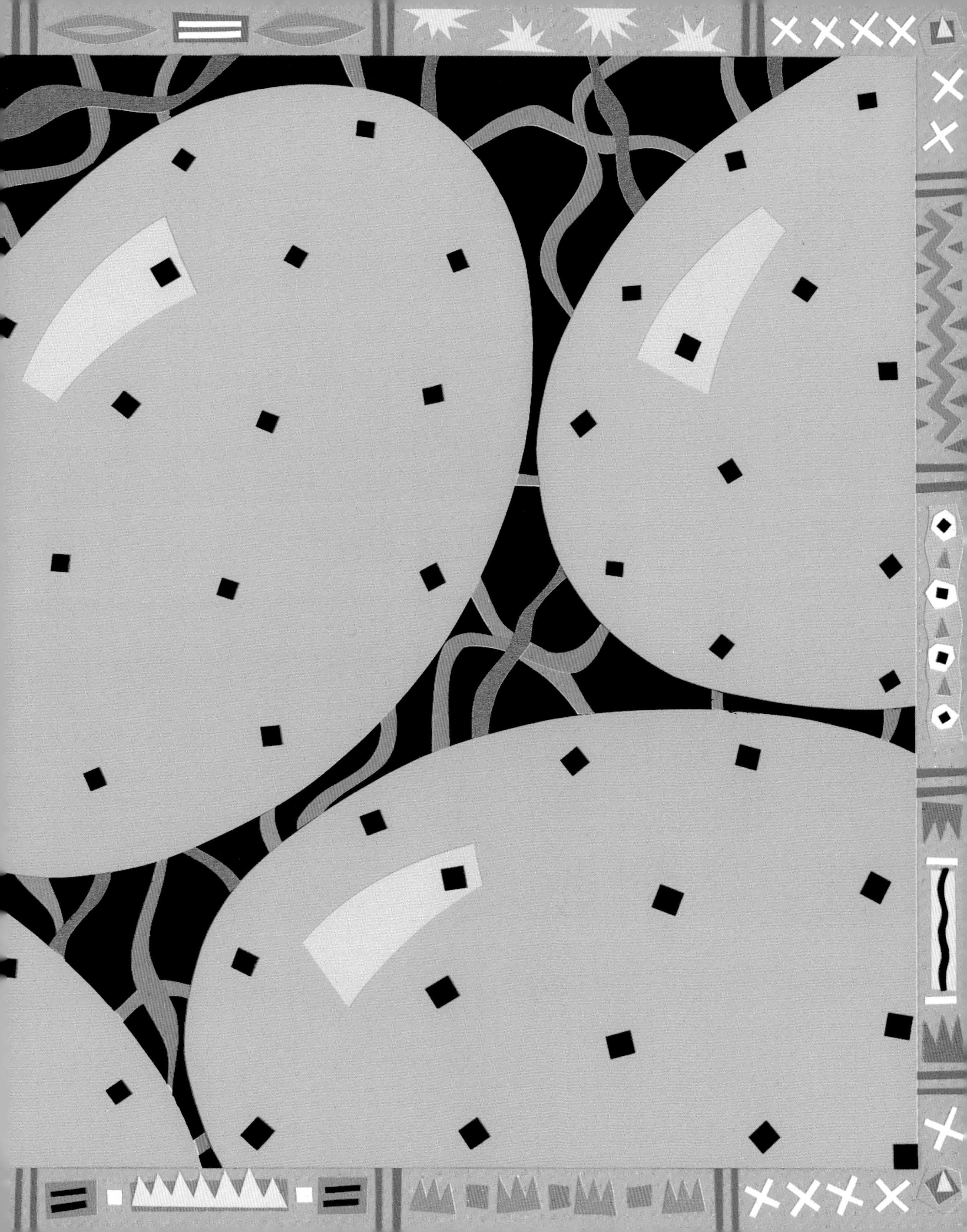

One day, Hawk came by. Hawk said to herself, "The person who owns this nest no longer cares for it. I will sit on those poor little eggs."

Hawk sat on the eggs.
She sat and sat and sat.
Nobody came to the nest.

The eggs began to hatch and no Crow came.
The little crows crept out of their shells, and Hawk flew about getting food for them.

The little crows got bigger and bigger, their feathers grew, their wings got strong, and Hawk fetched and carried for them all day long.

Crow was out and about one day
when suddenly she remembered
her nest and flew back to it.
There she found Hawk taking
care of the little crows.

"Hawk!" said Crow.
"What do you want?"
said Hawk.
"Give me back those little
crows!"
"Why?" said Hawk.
"Because they're mine,"
said Crow.

Hawk fluffed up her feathers and said, "You laid the eggs to be sure, but then you went off and left them.
I came by and sat on the nest. For many days, as I watched over the eggs, I didn't eat a thing. Since they hatched I've been working away to keep them fed. I'm not giving them back."

"Well, I'm taking them back!" said Crow.
"No, you won't," said Hawk. "Where were you when I was looking after your children? You're too late. They're staying with me."
"Very well," said Crow, "I shall take this matter to the King of the Birds and see what he has to say."

“Fine,” said Hawk. “Let’s go.”
So Crow and Hawk went to see
Eagle, King of the Birds.

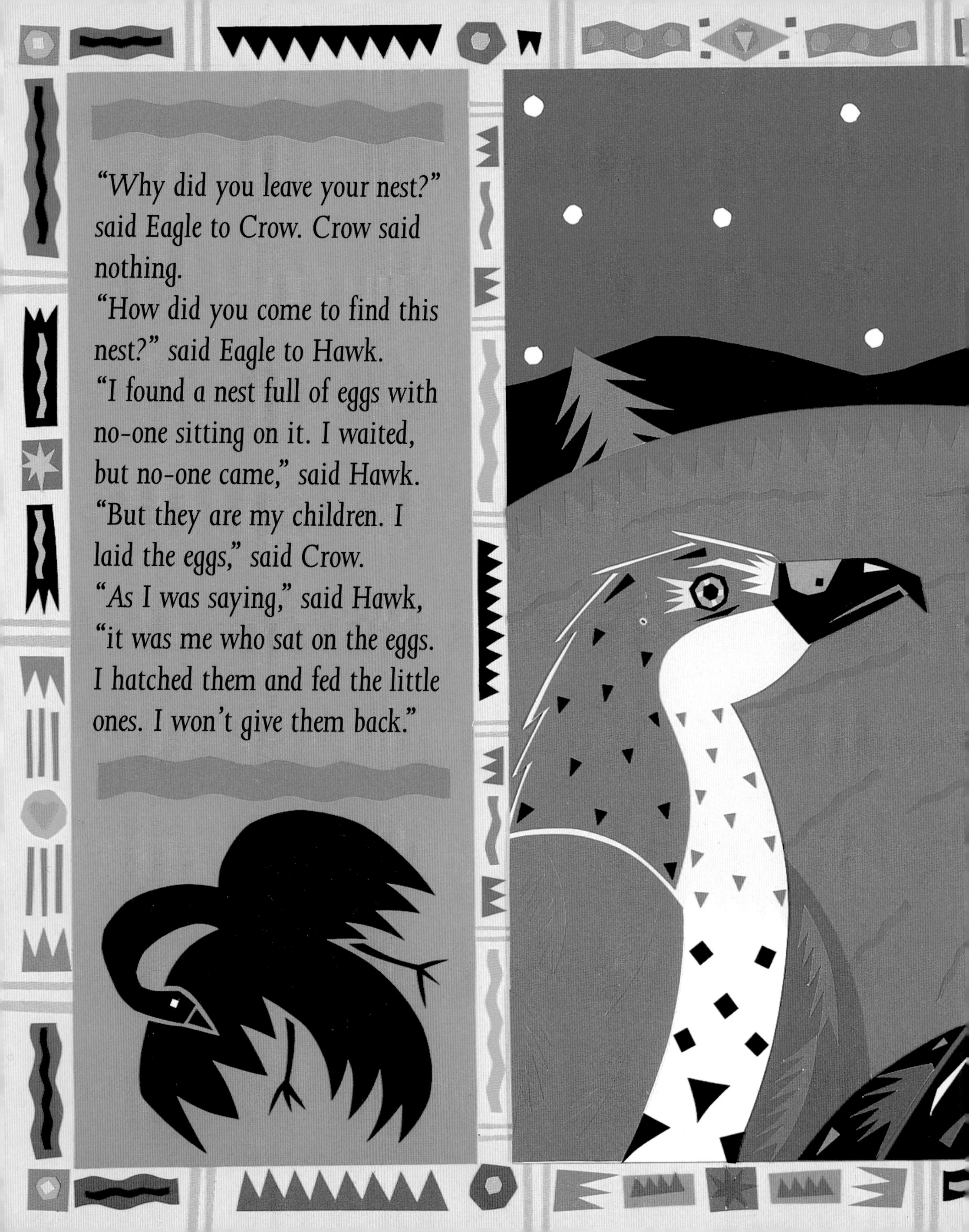

"Why did you leave your nest?" said Eagle to Crow. Crow said nothing.

"How did you come to find this nest?" said Eagle to Hawk.

"I found a nest full of eggs with no-one sitting on it. I waited, but no-one came," said Hawk.

"But they are my children. I laid the eggs," said Crow.

"As I was saying," said Hawk, "it was me who sat on the eggs. I hatched them and fed the little ones. I won't give them back."

Eagle spoke: "If you, Crow, really cared for your young ones, you wouldn't have left the nest. Hawk has been their mother."

Crow said, "King, ask the little ones which mother they want. *Ask* the little ones."

"*Well?*" said the Eagle to the little crows.

"Hawk is the only mother we know," they said.

"No, I am your real mother," said Crow.

"Oh no," said the little ones. "Hawk hatched us. Hawk fed us. You left us."

So that's how it was settled. The little crows stayed with Hawk. Crow began to weep.

"Don't cry," said Eagle. "This is the way it must be. You left the nest, you have lost the children."

And off went all the little crows with Hawk.